Secret Baby

Scott Wylder

Table of Contents:

Chapter 1

(Anastasia)

I took the job at Worthington Enterprises because it seemed like lucrative move. I could save up money to open my own catering business and before I turned thirty, I would be a business owner. But I ended up getting oh, so much more. More than I could have ever hoped for, more than I had ever imagined possible.

My boss, Ross Worthington, owned ten small businesses. He also owned a large retail business. He ran them all from his headquarters in Massachusetts. He was looking for someone creative to head the advertising department, and I just happened to have the right credentials.

Moving from Kansas as soon as I graduated college, I was new to the area and had been working at a local restaurant for a few months so I wouldn't dip into my savings account to pay rent and utilities and the like. I liked the job at the restaurant, but minimum wage was not cutting it, I needed better pay, if I ever intended to open my own business. World Cuisine Catering. It has a nice ring to it, I think.

Anyway, I went through several rounds of meetings and interviews before I met Ross. When I first laid eyes on him, my heart kicked into overdrive. He was the sort of suited, New England sexy that just demands attention wherever he goes. His short-cropped black hair and sapphire blue eyes that seemed to pierce right through me, was enough to garner my lusty desires. Add to that the confident swagger, the five-o'clock shadow, wide shoulders and narrow hips, and you have a volatile mixture.

I felt like a blathering fool during our first meeting, which he assured me was only a preliminary meeting so that we could just get to know each other a bit.

For the next interview I sat in his office in my best fancy office skirt and blouse suit, wishing I had worn my low-heeled black shoes instead of my slightly worn burnt-sienna flats that matched the accent colors in my skirt. He would be there any minute to conduct the formal interview. Just him and me. He told me at the informal meeting that the next interview would end with his hiring me, or thanking me for my time and interest, which meant I was not hired.

I had to impress him. But how do you impress a self-made billionaire? I was so nervous and nearly jumped out of my skin at every little noise.

Then Ross Worthington opened the door and walked in with a roguish grin on his face and a devilish twinkle in his eyes. My nerves didn't calm down, they died, right there on the spot. Frozen. That's how I sat, staring at him for several seconds as he approached me with his hand out, expecting a handshake.

Timidly, I shook his hand. His grip was firm and warm, the touch of his skin sending little tingles through my body and tightening my stomach. I collected myself and smiled back at him as he sat across the desk from me.

He was not the first gorgeous man I had ever met, but he was the first that I had thought, *I want him*, about. In high school, all the boys were immature jerks and I was not interested. I focused on my grades. In college, I had a few flings, but nothing more. I was centered on my future career as owner and operator of World Cuisine Catering. That left no time for boyfriends. It was not something that I ever thought much about—missing out on the dates and the sex never really bothered me.

Ross finished looking over the papers in his hand and laid them aside, turning that piercing gaze back to me. The interview consisted of only a few questions about my past experience, which was not much. I was honest with him even though I was tempted to embellish. I had taken the full course in advertising as a backup plan, just in case my dreams of the catering business flopped. My grades in those advertising and marketing classes were, as with all my other grades, superior. Many people could label me as many things, but never as a slacker. I had worked with a small company through college that needed help with their advertising and marketing department, and I gave the names and numbers as references on the Worthington Enterprise application.

"Miss Penland, it seems to me that you are right for the position here at Worthington Enterprises. You do understand that as head of the department, you will be working long hours and you will be the overseer for *all* adverts and marketing mock-ups for *all* my companies, correct?" Ross gave me a smile and nod.

Clearing my throat, wanting to jump up and squeal because he had more or less just hired me, I took a deep breath. My smile was uncontrollable. "Yes, sir. Long hours and a heavy workload never hurt me before. I would welcome the opportunity to work here, sir."

He laughed. "Okay, okay. You can stop being so formal and stop responding like an applicant. You can call me Ross, everybody does, except my mother but she doesn't work here, so we won't get into that." He chuckled again and shook my hand. "You, Anastasia Penland, are now, officially, the head of my main advertising and marketing department."

I stood, my knees trembled. "Thank you, sir, uhm, I mean, Ross." His name rolled off my tongue nicely. I liked the name Ross; strong, simple, sexy.

He opened the door and ushered me out first. "You do realize that if something goes wrong in any of the departments, it's your head on the chop-block."

That unnerved me. "I understand but what if it's something someone else screws up, not me? Will I still be held accountable?" I had never been a boss before, never had people working under my supervision, and I knew nothing of these new people I had yet to meet.

"Well, that's a different matter. If you're not the one who makes the mistake, then no." He touched my arm to stop me in mid-stride and opened a door on his right. "Here's your department. Let's meet your staff." He moved aside, holding the door and I brushed by him, feeling the warmth of his body so close to mine. "I would still hold you responsible for fixing the problem, though."

Nodding, I stepped into the room, electricity buzzing down my right side from his closeness.

"Here's your staff." He motioned to include all six cubicles in the large room. "There are six wonderful, creative, talented, and very argumentative people here."

"Only six?" I couldn't stop the question. I just blurted it out, shocked that there were only six people in charge of all marketing for eleven companies.

"Only six. I like to keep things simple, Miss Penland. Each of them will report directly to you, and you will report directly to me. See? Simple." He led me through the center of the room to another glass-fronted office and opened that door, also. "This is your office. Take today to set it up however you want it. Make a list of any equipment and furniture you will need, and I'll have it delivered in a few days."

Stepping into the office, *my* office, I felt like I had just made it. It was perfect. It was also very large, in my opinion. "You mean, I'm on the clock as of right now?"

Winking, he offered, "Unless you have more pressing appointments to see to, yes."

"Oh, no. Right now is fine. I just wasn't prepared for…" I waved my hand around the office and chuckled nervously.

"What? To get the job?" He wagged a finger back and forth, clucking his tongue. "Now, that's not a winning attitude, Miss Penland. Confidence is key in this world. Always be confident." He let his eyes slide over my body and I could feel it moving along, like hands caressing me.

"Yes, sir. Confidence." I nodded curtly, hoping my face wasn't red.

"Ross. Always Ross." He backed out of the office and shut the door.

Chapter 2
(Ross)

From our first meeting, I knew Anastasia Penland was going to be the new head of marketing here at Worthington Enterprises. With her jet-black hair, grey-green eyes, full lips, and perfectly curvy figure, how could I pass her up? She had the right credentials. She was young and full of life, full of ideas. She was exactly the type of person I needed in that position.

And she was exactly the person I wanted to get into other positions, too. Positions that had nothing to do with Worthington Enterprises.

I'm stuck in a loveless relationship with a woman I've been married to for ten years. There was no prenuptial agreement because I wasn't worth as much back then as I am now. She doesn't live with me. We haven't lived together in over six years. Most people think I'm single. Neither of us wears our rings and we have no mutual friends. She lives in her own house over an hour away and we don't speak. She lives her life and I live mine. Of course, she lives on my money.

She has her beaus, and I take on lovers. We have separate lives, except for the money. If I divorce her, she gets half of everything. She's heartless, ruthless, and has hated me for quite some time. I've often thought about divorcing her and giving her half but somehow, I just can't do that. It would be as if she were winning. That would make me the loser.

I don't like to lose. That's not how I became a self-made billionaire. Losing is not in my vocabulary. So, I'll remain a married man on paper, but I won't let her rule my life.

When I see something I want, I don't stop until I get it.

I want Anastasia. And I won't stop until I have her.

Making her head of marketing was only the first step.

I'll be spending loads of time alone with her in the office. She's going to be a very busy girl. She won't have time to think about having a relationship, but maybe she will be up for an office fling with the boss. I'll work my many charms and whittle away at her until she can't resist anymore. Then I'll show her the time of her young life, at my side and in my bed.

Hopefully, I can keep my hands off her until she's ready. I wanted to lock my office door and ravage her during the formal interview. If she knew of the thoughts going through my head, would she have taken the job? I'm not sure. I'll lock her into the job with a salary way above what a newbie should be making and then I'll see to it that she simply cannot spurn my advances.

I might be many things, but I know how people think. I know what drives them. Money is a grand manipulator for most people. I suspect that, being young and hoping to one day own her own business, it is also one of Anastasia's motivators in life.

Chapter 3

(Anastasia)

The salary Ross offered me was much more than I ever anticipated. With that salary, I could have my catering business up and running within a couple of years, still have my personal savings, plenty of money for daily expenses and bills, and a cushion for the business. As long as I kept my head on straight. I couldn't go wild and be frivolous with the money, but if I was careful, I would be set.

Three weeks into the new job, I had seen little of Ross. It was disappointing but made each of his visits all the more special. I worked hard to impress him. But that first month, I admit, was overwhelming. More often than not, I found myself still in my office at the dinner hour. The staff was great. And, just as Ross had bragged, they were very talented. They were work-oriented, too. And argumentative. That was fine with me. It kept the long days interesting. Besides, most artistic people are given to arguing—especially if they think you are insulting their work, or you want something major changed.

During my fifth week, I began to relax. I did not feel as much like the new employee anymore and was on friendly terms with all my staff. The rough edges were wearing off and we all began to get along much better. It was becoming an easy routine. I was accustomed to the long hours in the office and no longer felt drained all the time.

It was in that week that Ross called me into his office and made a pass at me. What would become one of many, many passes at me.

"Anastasia, we need to work a bit more on this ad for the Mangrove's Retail and Food store." He tapped a mock-up on the easel, stepped behind me, and pushed his office door shut.

"All right. What more did you have in mind for it?" I was confused. It seemed perfect to me.

"I was thinking, maybe a little more late-night, not so much mid-morning when all the mothers are watching kids shows mindlessly with their little ones. Does that make sense?" He cocked his head and looked me up and down.

My heart fluttered and stuttered under his unapologetic gaze. "I think so." Not really, but I did not want to just come out and say so. I wanted him to give an example, of his own volition.

He moved to stand directly in front of me, I had to look up to meet his eyes. He caressed my arm from shoulder to wrist seductively, staring into my eyes with hot passion. My thighs tensed, my nipples hardened, and I bit my lip to keep from moaning.

"More late night, when couples are lying naked in their warm and rumpled beds, encompassed in the afterglow of their lovemaking. You know, after they've shed their clothes, most likely in a hurry, leaving them on the floor, and worked up an appetite, gotten sweaty and dirty." He traced a finger from my earlobe to my collarbone.

I did moan a little that time. Couldn't stop it. No one had touched me like that in over a year. Trying to nod, I asked breathlessly, "What does all that have to do with Mangrove's?"

"Think about it. Couples in that state are soon going to be thinking about something to eat, there's the food department and the in-house, twenty-four-hour deli. They'll be wanting to shower, there's a plug spot for our personal health and beauty, the pharmacy, shampoo, you name it. Then these couples, always, always, will be thinking about how to dress, what will make them more appealing to their partner, what will be comfortable, affordable and still do all these? Our clothes, of course." He leaned close to my ear and said, "You gotta think outside the box, Anastasia." His deep voice rumbled sexily against my ear, tickling the hair that hung over it.

The sensation was out of this world alluring. I wanted to press my body to his right there but thought better of it. He was just making a point. Right? Then his hands slid from my shoulders all the way to my hips as he pulled back, no smile on his face, only sexual heat in his eyes. A wanton lust so powerful that I nearly swooned upon seeing it.

"Outside the box. Right. I'll get right on it, Ross." My voice was breathless, and the air suddenly seemed too hot in his office. I moved shakily toward the door, hoping he had not noticed his closeness had affected me.

He put his hand on the door, over my head, his body lightly touching me from shoulder to hip. "You don't have to start on it right away, Anastasia. We could...*talk* for a few minutes, go over some *ideas* first that way you have a better understanding of what I want from you." His voice held a lusty tone that, if we'd been in a bedroom, would have bent me to his every desire.

I didn't respond right away; I was unable to respond. Fighting the urge to press back against him, to feel more of him against me, I closed my eyes and stood still.

Then his lips lightly touched my neck just between my shoulder and earlobe.

I gasped. My instinct was to move forward, away from the unexpected touch, but the door blocked my getaway. I had to step backward to allow room for the door to open, but he was there, so close, kissing my neck so lightly, his breath as uneven as my own.

Shrinking to the side, I encountered his arm. His hand was still firmly planted on the door, my escape.

"Anastasia, stay for a while. It's private in here. The door has a lock and I could show you what I want from you."

His breath against my neck, the gentle movement of his lips there, I was done for, lost in my own lust for him. My desire to be touched, caressed, kissed, and naked against him overrode all my senses and I leaned into him, still unable to utter a word, and nodded.

The episode was hotter than hot. His hands were all over me, tugging at my clothes, gripping at my curves, tweaking my nipples under my shirt, with me pressed against the door. I untucked his shirt and put my hands on his chiseled chest. It was wonderful to have his naked skin under my hands, within my grasp. He was hard. All of him was hard. His erection stood out against the material of his suit pants. I touched him there and he gasped, drawing in a deep breath, holding it, and closing his eyes, he whispered, "Yes."

I gripped him through his pants, marveling at his size, wanting him inside me. All thoughts of propriety had withered and blown away from me. He worked up the hem of my skirt and pushed aside my wet panties. When his fingers touched me there, I thought my head would explode. I spread my legs and pressed my hips forward.

A loud, sharp knock on the door at my back ended our session abruptly and before either of us could gain an ounce of satisfaction. Panic seized me and I pushed him away, immediately finger-combing my hair back into place and straightening my clothes. He moved quickly, tucking his shirt back into his pants and sitting in his chair. He pushed up close to his desk and waited until I was seated before ushering in the visitor.

"Come in!" He sounded irritated. No wonder, that close and being interrupted, I was irritated, too.

It was his secretary, Julian. She stepped in and looked from me to Ross and back again, a small smile playing at her mouth. Not the happy kind of smile, but the kind that is more of a smirk, degrading in its knowledge of what was going on.

She handed him a list across the desk and cut a sharp, knowing look at me. Then she spoke to Ross, "These plans need to be finalized." She glanced at me and winked at him. "Whenever you finish here. We can't move forward without your great big..." She giggled and then continued, "...*signature*, Ross." She spun on her heel and rolled her eyes at me as she exited the room. The door shut with a loud bang.

Chapter 4

(Ross)

The first time I kissed Anastasia's neck, I hadn't meant to do it. Really. I just sort of lost control. It was a heady feeling, but afterward, I was angry at myself for not having more willpower than that.

When her dainty, soft hands touched my bare chest, I wanted to bend her over and give her the fucking of her life. Then she squeezed my cock and even though it was through my pants, I wanted to rip off her clothes, bury that hard rod in her softness, in her soft, *wetness*. Over and over again.

Then Julian ruined it. Yes, Julian and I used to play around at the office. I never felt about her the way I do about Anastasia, it was more of a mutually beneficial relationship. Julian needs sex often, and I had been willing to give it to her. It would have been the same with any guy there, though, if I had not been the one to first take Julian up on her wanton flirting. It was so hot that it burned out as quickly as a flash-fire for us. We both lost interest in a matter of three months.

I wanted to make sure that didn't happen with Anastasia.

And, it did not.

We had been carrying on at the office for well over three months when I first invited her to my place to spend a weekend. I thought things were getting serious enough between us that I should come clean about my marriage.

The first night, I couldn't bring myself to do it. All I wanted to do that night was her. It was a long and glorious night that forever embedded her in my heart and mind. That night I fell in love with Anastasia. All the next day, we spent in bed, enjoying each other's bodies. I was exhausted by that night, and so, put off telling her again. The rest of the weekend passed, and she was still in the dark about my wife, Sheila.

Feeling bad about it, I planned on having another special weekend with Anastasia in which I would come clean. She had been working for me for almost six months, and during that time had quickly become my only love interest. She was a mid-western mystery to me. What burned in her heart for me? Did she long only for sex? Or money? Or was she so wrapped up in her dreams that I was only a fling to be forgotten the moment she opened her new business?

I was clueless as to her feelings for me.

Highly suspecting, and greatly hoping, that she felt the same about me as I did about her, I gave up my darkest secret during a weekend getaway at a seaside resort where all the rich and famous people stay in New England.

At first, she was pissed, and I didn't blame her one bit. I would have been furious had the tables been turned. But not Anastasia, my sweet, kind, sexy, minx with the true heart of gold. She forgave me within the hour. Her entire mood changed. I was elated. She knew about my conundrum with my on-paper wife and was still willing to be with me.

Our exploits at work became more passionate but never seemed to last as long as before. And something about the way she looked at me had changed. Maybe she had trouble trusting me after learning about Sheila. Whatever it was, she seemed to be working through it and she kept accepting my advances.

Then, one day, I invited her to my place. Winter was closing in. I had bought her a gift and wanted her to have it before the first cold blast of the New England winter.

She arrived in her own car, never took a hired car at all, that one.

I greeted her at the front door. "Hello, beautiful. I'm glad you could make it." We kissed and I was immediately aroused.

"I wouldn't miss it, Ross." She hung her light jacket by the door and followed me to the downstairs den where I'd laid a nice low fire in the hearth.

"Sit here. I'll fix us a drink and I have something for you that I think you'll love." Smiling, feeling like a teenager with his first serious crush, I walked away to make the drinks and get her gift.

She seemed happy when I handed her the gift and tore the box open. She sat staring at the beautiful thigh-length coat, with no expression at all. Well, I thought she was shocked at the expensive gift and I chuckled as I took a seat by her side. She turned to me with a look I'll never forget.

"Ross, I can't accept this. It's too much." She folded the tissues back over the coat and replaced the lid and set it on the coffee table, not making eye contact.

"Don't be silly!" I laughed again. "It's not like I can't afford to buy you expensive gifts."

She stood abruptly and moved quickly to the door to retrieve her own jacket. I ran to catch up to her.

"What's wrong? Don't you like it? I can take it back, buy you one that you like, baby. Where are you going?"

"It's lovely, Ross. But I can't accept it. Please, I need to go, I don't feel so well."

She gave me a quick kiss and as she stood back, waiting for me to move away from the door so she could leave, I noted that she did indeed look paler than normal and her cheeks carried a warm glow high on her cheekbones. She assured me that she did not want or need me or anyone else to look after her, and then she left.

She refused my calls for the weekend. I left a ton of voicemails. So many that her phone stopped taking those, too. I was worried that she had come down with something serious, and I went to her place.

I had only been there once, we much preferred my place to her little apartment for our rendezvous. But I knew where it was and saw no reason to stay away. I couldn't stand the thought that she was in bed too sick to even answer the phone for two whole days.

When I arrived, I went straight to her door and knocked. No answer. I knocked several more times before I thought to peek through the little window.

Her apartment was empty. There was no sign that she had ever lived there.

Her cell rang endlessly and then disconnected.

At work, I searched for her. No one had heard anything from her at all, she just hadn't shown up that morning.

Dejected and worried sick, I went to my office. There was a letter on my desk. I opened it, expecting nothing in particular and then realized it was from Anastasia.

The gist of the letter was that I shouldn't search for her. She had returned to Kansas and didn't want to be bothered. Then she thanked me for the opportunity to work for my company and all the experiences it gave her.

There were no words of love or even of longing. She signed it with her full name.

The end.

Did she know that I could never leave her alone? Did she realize that she had just turned my whole world upside-down?

I don't like to lose.

Chapter 5

(Anastasia)

Finding out that Ross was *technically* married almost crushed me. I had started falling in love with him. I know. That was stupid on my behalf. Our relationship had started as an office fling, nothing more. In the beginning, we thought of each other as friends with benefits. That suited me just fine. In the beginning.

Then he invited me to his place. Then he started taking me out on the town, showing me good times in the high life that were more befitting a girlfriend-boyfriend relationship. Then Julian started chatting me up every chance she got, trying to pump me for information about me and Ross. I held my own. I have been around females like her since high school. It was when she started telling me about her and Ross's office fling that I realized I was developing serious feelings for him because my instant reaction was jealousy.

I didn't show her that I was jealous, though. That would have been akin to putting blood in a shark tank. She would have eaten me alive with more and more detailed stories about her and Ross—I definitely didn't need that.

Around that time, I got sick. It was a struggle to get out of bed in the mornings and drag myself to work. Even the prospect of seeing Ross, and having sex in his office, the risky business that used to set my libido ablaze, no longer appealed to me. Nevertheless, I dragged myself along, acting as normally as possible, thinking all the time that the illness would pass in time.

But it did not pass. It got worse.

I had my suspicions long before I made an appointment at the clinic. I just needed the bloodwork to confirm those suspicions. And the bloodwork definitely confirmed it. I was pregnant.

With this discovery, I did the only thing I could do…I packed up and moved back to Kansas. I left a note for Ross, but I didn't tell him about the baby. What was he going to do? Jump up and down for joy? Have a celebration? No. He was married. Even if they were living separate lives, the man was still married.

No way was I even going to consider abortion or giving up the baby for adoption. Nope. I considered telling Ross on my last visit to his house, but I could not do it. So, I packed up and left, practically overnight. I gave no notice at work, told none of my staff that I was leaving, I left no forwarding address, and changed my phone number. I just left. Disappeared.

Driving back to Kansas, I cried until my eyes were swollen and my face was puffy and bright pink. I had to get it out of my system. I had a baby to think about and prepare for. I had our futures to consider.

It was time to go balls-to-the-wall with opening my own business. It had to be a success, or I would not get another chance.

***

Almost four years later, my little girl, Leslie, had just had the bestest birthday ever. She was a beautiful little raven-haired gift. Looking at her, tired and content after her birthday party, made my heart sing. She was the best thing that ever happened to me.

She was also a daily reminder of her father, Ross Worthington. Some days I missed him and our wild lovemaking, the feelings I had for him, and the way he looked at me. After nearly four years, though, I thought about him less and less. It had gotten to the point that I hardly ever thought about him, and rarely pined for his caresses.

There were other men. None of whom were father material, though. They were flash-fire romances that burned out way before I ever thought about making one permanent.

My catering business, Worldwide Cuisine, was a booming success. I did business almost solely online. I liked the new, updated name, it left a lot of room for possible catering requests. Especially since the business had grown immensely and I had companies in Kansas, Nebraska, Wyoming, and was working on two locations in Missouri. There was a lot of international peoples in those states.

When Leslie laid down for her nap after the party, I made a pot of coffee and sat at my computer to check on my local business.

There was only one request that day. It was from a company, W&P. Their newest installment of the large retail store would be opening in my area soon. W&P wanted my company to cater a party for their executives and owners beforehand.

Without a second thought, I replied with the catering list, the price list, the timeframe, and other pertinent paperwork that needed to be filled out before I could start on the job. It usually took about a week for people to get everything in order and get it back to me. So, I let it go, didn't spend much time thinking about that job in particular. I was raising a three-year-old by myself and overseeing several small catering companies that were spread throughout the Midwest. To say the least, I was very busy.

Two days later, the paperwork had been returned to my email. The date for the party was only three weeks away. I had special orders for food to get done and had to hire more servers and cooks to help with the event.

The day of the event came, and I was on-site setting up the tables. There was a flurry of activity, people bustling around, my twenty employees plus the twenty or more who were decorating the place, plus all the execs and owners who were milling around just being nosy. Just seeing how the other half lives, I suppose.

They were getting on my nerves, so I took a break and went outside to get some fresh air and elbow room. A car pulled around to the side of the building. I thought I saw Ross in that car. For just a split second, I was sure it was his handsome face peering out the back window in my direction.

Then the car was out of sight.

I wandered around outside for a few minutes and then went back to the second floor and entered the melee again. Two hours later, I was in the makeshift kitchen, cooking the entrees for the meal.

Sweat slithered down from my hairline into my face, my clothes stuck to me, my other three cooks worked just as hard as I did. We were all quickly becoming exhausted. Just as I was at my grossest, a man walked into the little crowded kitchen and propped against the far wall. Glancing up at him, wondering why the hell a suit would be in the kitchen, I kept cooking. It took almost a full minute before my heat-exhausted brain realized who he was.

Ross Worthington stood in the steamy kitchen, all cool and sexy, leaning against the wall. Watching me with an odd expression, he moved toward me.

My heart nearly stopped. I was so not ready to face him. I had left Massachusetts to avoid him.

Chapter 6

(Ross)

After nearly four years of not seeing her, I was shocked when I saw Anastasia standing over the stove, cooking for the execs of my newest store. Granted, I had chosen the location because I knew that's where Anastasia was from originally, and I had hoped to bump into her, or find her again. In all those years, I never got her out of my mind. Or out of my broken heart.

She left without saying goodbye; she just ran away, and she never told me why. Never told anyone why, as far as I knew. One day our relationship was blossoming into something much bigger, much more permanent, and the next day, she was gone.

As I approached her, I had a mixture of feelings swirling inside me. I was upset, happy, angry, excited, and scared. Yes, scared that she would reject me outright, scared that in my absence she had gotten married.

I had planned for that moment when we met again. All the things I would say, do, the way I would act. Yeah, right. That went out the window as soon as I spied her sweat-soaked self in that humid little excuse for a kitchen.

"Anastasia?" I had to be certain it was her. With her hair pulled tightly away from her face, and in a uniform and apron, it was a bit difficult to tell for sure. My eyes said maybe it was her and my heart said it was her.

She stopped cooking and looked at me. "Yes?" She leaned forward a bit. "Oh, my God. Ross? Is that you?"

Laughing, I nodded. "It is. Fancy seeing you here. So Worldwide Cuisine is *your* business?"

She nodded and smiled. "Yes, it is. And I take it that W&P is yours?"

"Indeed. So, you look busy, could we talk later?" I tried to keep an even keel although my emotions were running from one end of the spectrum to the other.

She averted her gaze and began cooking again. Her answer was short and left no doubt in me that she knew what I wanted to talk about. It also left me with no doubt that she wasn't thrilled about it.

"Sure. Seven tonight." She turned back to cooking and away from me without waiting for a response. She was busy and wanted to be left to her job. I respected that and left her alone.

It was the most difficult dinner party I had ever sat through. The minutes and hours ticking by as I listened to the drivel being spouted by the attendees and all the while knowing that Anastasia, the love of my life, was only a few yards away. I wanted to go to her. At the same time, I thought with the way she reacted to me earlier that it might be a very bad idea. Nevertheless, I found myself leaving the after-dinner party at half past six.

Anastasia was just leaving the kitchen when I entered. Had she been about to run out, run away from me again?

"Anastasia! Hey, wait up!" I hurried through the room and to the door where she waited impatiently.

"I have a lot to do still. There's cleaning and packing up the equipment. I have to help them, Ross, I really don't have time for a chit-chat right now." She turned to walk away.

Taking hold of her arm, I turned her back to me. "You're the one who suggested seven as our meeting time." I looked around and saw that most of the equipment, hers anyway, had already been removed. "It looks like all your things have already been taken out. You wouldn't be trying to avoid me, would you?" I grinned, hoping to sound playful, not like it hurt me to know she was trying to run away again.

"No, I'm not." She sighed and rolled her eyes, ran her hand over her hair, and gave me an exasperated look.

"Listen, I just don't think us talking right now is a good idea. I mean, really, do you?"

She had never faltered in her words to me. She had always been articulate and intelligent. "Well, yes, I do think it's a good idea. I think you owe me an explanation for the way you left, Anastasia." There it was out, and I couldn't take it back. That wasn't how I had wanted to say it, but it worked all the same.

She turned to me with all trace of good humor gone. "No, Ross, I do not owe you any explanation. You are a married man, remember? We were no more than an office hookup, and an occasional weekend hookup. So, you took me out on the town—no more than you'd do for an expensive call-girl. So, no, I do *not* owe you an explanation." She pulled away from my light grip and stomped off toward the elevators.

My heart was crushed. Had she really felt that way about all I had done for her? That I considered her no more than an expensive call-girl? Where had I gone so wrong with her?

Taking an elevator, I tried to catch up to her, but she was gone by the time I reached the parking lot. Her employees who were still packing up one of the catering trucks, would not give me a shred of information about their boss. In a way, I was glad—that meant they wouldn't be apt to give out personal information about her to anyone, and that was good. On the other hand, I was furious. Couldn't they see that I loved her, or I would not have been out there begging for information about her?

Finally, one of the younger women said, "Hey, mister. Don't worry about it. She wasn't really giving you the brush-off, she just had to go pick up her kid at the sitters. She'll be home in a little while. Call her." She jumped into the truck and the driver drove away.

Looking from W&P to the road and back again, I tried to digest what the girl had just told me. Anastasia had a kid.

That sealed the deal. There was no way she would come back to me. She already had her life, her *family*, in Kansas. Her business was doing well. What more could she want? Definitely not a reminder of an *office hookup*, as she had so indelicately put it.

I went back to the party, making excuses and apologies for running out. I wooed the guests and drowned my aching heart with too much booze.

That night, I slept it off in a hotel with a call-girl, a hooker, if you will. Not my finest moment, but what did I have to lose? Not Anastasia. She was obviously already long gone and out of my reach for good.

As Candy left the next morning, I realized that I had been living restricted since Anastasia left. I had lived as if I thought she would be back. I had taken lovers, but none of those relationships were anything other than sex for the sake of sex. I am still a man and I needed sex to remain healthy and partially content.

Besides, Anastasia had taken at least one lover—she had a kid to prove that point.

All day, I kept seeing images of Anastasia naked, riding some crude, dirty cowboy type. It was the setting, I'm sure. The Midwest landscapes. The images in my head unlocked all the pent-up anger and hurt that I had kept locked away for nearly four years.

The hotel room never stood a chance. I destroyed it in a fit of rage and jealousy.

I have never been jealous of anyone in my entire life. Until that moment. I was horribly jealous over Anastasia. She had been mine. No one else had a right to see her naked, to touch her delicious curves, or taste the sweet nectar of her sex.

My flight back to Massachusetts was set to depart the next morning but I stayed in Kansas. I wasn't sure what

I planned to accomplish other than paying for the damage I had caused to the hotel room. Leaving without talking to Anastasia was not an option for me at that point.

I would find her, and we would talk it out until I was satisfied.

Chapter 7

(Anastasia)

Thinking that Ross had surely returned to Massachusetts, my surprise was great when, a week after the event at W&P, I answered a knock at my front door to find Ross standing there.

With Leslie on my hip, I gawked at him. His sexy five-o'clock shadow had grown grizzled and made him seem haggard. His eyes were bloodshot and had dark circles under them. I had dark circles of my own from not sleeping well the last week. His unexpected appearance at the event had reawakened my feelings for him. Feelings that I had just gotten somewhat under control in the last few months.

We stared at each other for several seconds, both speechless.

Leslie put her hands on my face and turned me toward her. "Who that, Mommy?" She pointed one, tiny finger at her father.

Tears sprang to my eyes. "His name is Ross, honey." I had never thought the day would come when all three of us were in the same room together. Father, mother, daughter. And I was the only one who knew. I could keep the secret from both of them, or I could share it. I was torn over what to do.

Ross stuck out his hand and smiled, it was Leslie's smile. "Hello, little lady. I'm Ross. What's your name?"

Would he recognize his eyes and his smile mirrored back at him from his daughter's face?

"Leslie. Leslie LeighAnn Penland." She shook his hand, giggling.

"It's nice to make your acquaintance, Leslie LeighAnn Penland." He chuckled and looked back to me.

"I'm sorry, Ross, but I'm really very—"

"Very busy. I can see that you are, Anastasia. I just want to talk for a few minutes and then I'll leave you two lovely ladies to the rest of your day." He winked at Leslie and she giggled again. He smiled broadly.

Casting about in my mind for excuses, I found none. It was either let him in and get it over with, or possibly have to deal with him again at a later date, which I surmised would only be worse for all of us.

"Fine. But only for a few minutes. It's nearly time for an afternoon nap, isn't it, Leslie?" I nuzzled her cheek.

"No!" She laughed and covered her cheek.

"Oh, but, yes, it is." I let her down to run and play in the den, where most of her favorite toys were kept and then motioned Ross inside. "Let's sit in the dining room. Would you like something to drink?"

"Water would be fantastic. I feel like I've tried to swallow the Gobi Desert all of a sudden." He chuckled shortly.

He was nervous. I was glad. It helped cover my own nervousness. I got us both bottled waters and showed him to the dining room. "What's on your mind, Ross?"

Eyeing the room and what he could see of the property, he said, "You've done well for yourself. Or, your husband and you have done well, I should say." He nodded toward the den, indicating Leslie.

"There's no husband. And, thank you. I've tried." How long would it take him to inquire about Leslie's age? How long before something she said or did, made him think of himself? With him sitting across from me, I wasn't so sure that I ever wanted to tell him the truth, but I was also unsure what explanation I would give Leslie when she was older. She would have questions about her father, naturally, but what answers could I possibly give her? That he was an unknown? That he was a fling? That he was an office hook-up every now and then? That her mommy was wild back in the day and got pregnant by accident? No. I would have to do better than that.

"No husband?" His brow wrinkled as he looked back to the den where Leslie was riding a stick-horse back and forth by the doorway.

I shook my head. "Just me."

A bark of laughter escaped him, and he quickly covered it with a fake cough.

"What? Why do you think that's funny?" Instantly on the defensive, I sat forward, ready to ask him to leave.

Waving his hands in mock surrender, he replied, "I don't. I was just wondering if it was immaculate conception, since there's no husband." He grinned roguishly.

My heart fluttered at that grin. Oh, how far that very same grin had gotten him when I was with him. "No. Being a smartass will get you thrown out quick." His humor brought a smile, an unwanted one at that, to my face and I took another drink of my water to hide it.

He sobered and cleared his throat. "I'm sorry. It just struck me as funny."

Nodding, I set down my water. "So, what is it exactly that brings you unannounced to my door?"

"I wanted to let you know that I divorced Sheila not even a month after you…*left*…so suddenly." He seemed to bite back on the word, as if he had more to add to it but didn't.

Tingles covered me from head to toe. "Well, that's just lovely for you, I guess. But I thought you'd never do it. You said she would get half of everything." If I had stayed, would he have still divorced her? Had I screwed up by leaving so soon? By not telling him that he was a father? My stomach rolled over.

"She did. Half of everything that I had while we were married. That's why I'm opening several new stores, W&P." His words trailed off.

"Rebuilding the fortune, eh?" I scoffed. Of course he was. What else would he be doing in Kansas? Searching for me? Not likely.

Leslie ran in with her stick-horse. "You wanna ride Sally-Jo? I got her for my burfday." She held out the stick-horse to him and my heart twisted. A sob caught in my throat. To see them interacting was almost more than my rollercoaster emotions could handle.

"Aren't you afraid I'll be too heavy for Sally-Jo? I'd hate to break your birthday present." He smiled lovingly at her. He seemed so at ease with her. I had never thought of him as the fatherly type. The roguish, rich, playboy type was more fitting with my mental image and memories of him.

"No, silly, she's a pretend horsey." Leslie giggled, tilted her head to the side and for a moment, she and Ross looked so similar. A tear slipped from my eye and I quickly stood, swiped it away, and walked to a window just to have an excuse to turn my back on the scene.

"Well, how about if I promise to take her for a ride in a little while? I need to finish talking to your mommy right now. Is that okay, Leslie?"

"Sure. You talk funny."

Spinning, I said, "Leslie LeighAnn! That wasn't nice. Apologize to Mr. Worthington."

"His name is Ross." She held Sally-Jo close in a hug.

"Apologize to Ross, then." I wouldn't allow bad manners. I had taught her better and expected better but I knew she was talking about Ross's distinct Massachusetts accent.

She turned to him, looking at his feet. "Sorry, Ross. But you do talk funny." She ran back toward the den.

Ross laughed loudly. He held up a hand to me. "It's okay. It's my accent, I'm sure."

I sat at the table again, suddenly more mentally exhausted than I had been since finding out I was pregnant with Leslie.

"Why did you leave, Anastasia?" His voice was low, deep, and touched my heart. "You must have known that I loved you."

"Loved me? No, I did not know. Never even suspected. You were married and carrying on an office romance with the new girl, Ross. That's not what I would call love." I didn't realize I was yelling until Leslie ran to me and held up her arms.

I picked her up, fighting tears again, fighting the urge to yell more at Ross. How could I have ever known he was even thinking of love? It's not like he ever told me. The real reason it angered me so much to hear it from him was that I had been falling in love with him just before I left. Had he told me how he felt, I might have stayed. Our family might not have been separated.

"How could you think otherwise?" His voice was full of tension, he was keeping it cool because of Leslie.

"Mommy, I love you!" She wrapped her arms around my neck and squeezed tightly.

"I love you, too, sweetie. Always and forever." I hugged her back.

Ross stood. "I had planned on telling you the day I gave you the coat. I wanted it to be a special weekend away from everything and everybody when I bared my heart." He waved a hand over his head. "But then, you were gone. And now…" His eyes cut to Leslie and he stopped speaking.

There it was. The proverbial lightbulb had just turned on in his head. I held my breath and stood, holding Leslie tight and staring at him over her head.

He looked at me, his mouth dropped open and then it shut. He did this a few times, looking like a fish out of water. Pulling out the chair, he sat again. He pointed to Leslie and raised his eyebrows in question.

"What, Ross?" I wasn't giving up the information just yet. At that moment, I was more scared than I had ever been.

"Anastasia, is she?" There was a sadness in his voice.

"It's Leslie's nap time, Ross." I hurried up the stairs. Leslie waved to him over my shoulder.

"Bye, Ross." I felt her wave at him and I heard the sob catch in his throat as I cleared the last riser and disappeared from his sight.

Chapter 8

(Anastasia)

Back downstairs, I stood opposite Ross, the table between us.

Without looking at me, he asked, "How old is Leslie?"

It was time to come clean about it. With no delay, I answered, "She just turned three."

Ross sat quietly for a moment, looked at me, and nodded. "Why didn't you tell me, Anastasia?" The anger I had expected, was absent. Instead, he looked sadder than the saddest man on earth. The circles under his eyes were suddenly darker, his cheeks hollower, the set of his shoulders more dejected.

"How could I, Ross? You were married and had told me that you'd never give her a divorce. How was I to know you'd even care?"

"Because I did care! I do care! I still love you, Anastasia. All these years, I haven't been able to keep you off my mind." He made a mournful sound and rubbed his face. "I have a daughter?"

He looked to me for confirmation. I nodded tightly.

"I have a daughter." His eyes brimmed with tears. "*We* have a daughter. A beautiful, intelligent, little daughter, Anastasia."

"Yes, I suppose *we* do." Tears slipped down my cheeks.

Still half-expecting him to become irate at some point, I was happy to learn that he was only upset that he had not told me of his true feelings sooner. He very much wanted to be in my and Leslie's lives.

***

(Ross)

Finding out that I had a daughter…well, that changed the world for me. I was in love with Anastasia, but I loved her even more after learning that she had given birth to our child. There was no way I was going back to live in Massachusetts.

Visiting Anastasia and Leslie every chance I had over the next two months, I was the happiest I ever remember being in my life.

One evening, after a lovely homemade dinner with my two ladies, we were in the backyard drinking coffee as Leslie played with Sally-Jo. The sun was setting, casting amber hues all across the land. Anastasia had never looked more beautiful to me than she did sitting there with windblown hair and dressed in jeans and a tee-shirt.

"Anastasia?" I set my coffee aside.

"Yes?" Her voice held a dreamy tone as she watched the sunset.

"I want us to be together."

She turned to me, smiling.

"Forever. I want us to be together forever. I love you. I love our daughter." I moved closer and leaned in for a kiss.

"Forever is a very long time, Ross." She kissed me.

"I know. I want it to be. I'm not going back to Massachusetts. I've already looked into buying property right here."

"What? How can you not go back? That's where you conduct all your business from." Her shocked expression was nearly comical.

"Where there's a will, there's a way. There's no law that says I have to run my businesses from the Massachusetts location. I can move my base of operations, my headquarters, if you will, right out here eventually. Until then, I can manage with the occasional trip out there, I believe." Hoping she would have more to say about it than what she had, I waited.

Studying me for several long moments, she finally turned her attention back to the westering sun and our Leslie. It was an iconic picture forever burned into my mind's eye. Leslie with her long black hair flying out behind her as she rode the stick-horse and laughed. The multi-colored sky with the sun riding low toward the horizon setting the whole landscape ablaze with hues of orange, red, and yellow.

Taking out my cell phone, I snapped a few quick pictures of the scene and then recorded a video. Without realizing it, I had just been introduced to the wonders and love of fatherhood. The need to snap pictures, capture precious moments had just been born in me and would never die.

Chapter 9

(Anastasia)

Ross didn't get his answer that day. The way I saw it, he never really asked me a question. He was only doling out statements.

We started dating like a real couple the next week, though. We had play dates with Leslie and then we had our dates, just for us. My life was coming back together. My *family* was coming together.

It's not like I made plans for marriage, but the possibility is still out there and if I ever do get married, it would be to Ross.

Watching the sunset became a thing for us as a family. Leslie playing in the big backyard and the sun getting lower and lower as Ross sat with his arm around my shoulders, usually we drank coffee then. We didn't talk much, just took in the peace and serenity of the day's end. It was lovely.

Then, tucking Leslie in for the night became a regular part of our days together and she came to expect a story and a kiss from Ross.

One night, after he finished reading her a bedtime story, and kissed her goodnight, she looked up at him sleepily and asked, "Are you my daddy, Ross? I want you to be my daddy."

Standing in the doorway, my heart filled to bursting with love for that crafty, smart little girl. And, Ross handled the situation like a pro, never missing a beat.

"Well, Leslie, I am your father, as a matter of fact. I'm glad you want me to be your daddy, because I love being your daddy." He kissed her forehead. "I love you, Leslie."

"I love you, Daddy." She yawned and cuddled with her teddy bear, ready for sleep.

Ross met me in the hallway. "Kids are so adaptable." He reached for me, his fingers touching the back of my neck gently.

"Mm-hm. That they are." I let him pull me close for a passionate kiss.

"Maybe we should take a lesson from her, huh?" He devoured me with his eyes and walked me to the bedroom.

"Lesson?" I was unbuttoning his shirt. It had been so long since I'd touched his skin. I was starving for his touch.

"Being adaptable and accepting of…well…anything." He pulled my shirt over my head and tossed it to the floor, kicked the door shut, and took off my bra and dropped it as he guided me toward the bed.

Picking me up, he carried me the last few feet, tossed me roughly to the bed and yanked off my jeans and panties. I squealed with delight at his assertiveness. His desire was a turn-on for me. I arched my back and rubbed my breasts for him as he stepped out of the rest of his clothes.

"Come give me something to accept, Ross," I purred.

He climbed on the bed and I spread my legs, welcoming him back. His member was erect and throbbing as he pressed it against me, moving his hips side to side, rubbing me in the most erotic way.

I moaned as he took my nipple into his mouth, teasing it with his teeth and tongue. "I want you inside me, Ross," I pleaded.

"Forever?" He poised, ready for penetration.

"Forever," I answered as he guided himself into me.

The first round of lovemaking was rough and we both came quickly. The second round was more for our soul's satisfaction and it lasted for an hour. The sweet, slow strokings of our bodies against one another, turned the bedroom into our heaven for a while.

We lay in a tangle of arms and legs, still joined together, and drifted to sleep in the afterglow.

This would be our future.

This would be our forever.

END

Made in the USA
Middletown, DE
27 September 2019